Love Is in the Air

To Sacha, Tom, Malo, and Tara.
V.T.

Thank you, thank you, thank you, a thousand times and again
thank you to Alexis, Bâ-Lé, Carine, Clément, Damien, Élodie, Élise,
Emeline, Éric, Frédéric, Inès, Julien, Ludovic, Marietta, Olivier,
Romain, and Vincent!
V.T.

Published in 2009 by Windmill Books, LLC
303 Park Avenue South Suite # 1280, New York, NY 10010-3657

Adaptations to North American edition © 2009 Windmill Books
Copyright © 2006 Editions Milan, 300 rue Léon Joulin - 31101 Toulouse Cedex 9, France.

CREDITS:
Author: Amélie Sarn
Illustrator: Virgile Trouillot and Olivier Ducrest
A concept by Frédéric Puech and Virgile Trouillot based on an idea from Jean de Loriol.
Copyright © PLANETNEMO

Publisher Cataloging Information

Sarn, Amélie
          Love is in the air / Amélie Sarn ; illustrations by Virgile Trouillot and
Olivier Ducrest.
                    p. cm. – (Groove High)
          Summary: Zoe, Lena, Tom, and Ed are convinced there are two romances in
progress at Groove High—Groove Team member Vic and the boy she has a crush on,
and the school's director Iris Berrens and Khan, the handsome yoga teacher.
          ISBN 978-1-60754-212-4. – ISBN 978-1-60754-213-1 (pbk.)
ISBN 978-1-60754-214-8 (6-pack)
          1.   Secrecy—Juvenile fiction   2. Dance schools—Juvenile fiction
3. Boarding schools—Juvenile fiction   [1. Secrets—Fiction   2. Dance schools—
Fiction   3. Boarding schools—Fiction   4. Schools—Fiction   5. Friendship—Fiction]
I. Trouillot, Virgile   II. Ducrest, Olivier   III. Title   IV. Series
          [Fic]—dc22

Manufactured in the United States of America

Groove High

Amélie Sarn

Love Is in the Air

Illustrations by Virgile Trouillot
and Olivier Ducrest

Skyview Books

an imprint of

WINDMILL
BOOKS
New York

Me, I'm Zoe. I'm 14 years old and I'm following my dream: to go to Groove High to become a choreographer!

Vic: My best friend. Beautiful, blonde, always on the cutting edge of fashion, and super fun to be around.

Lena: Athletic, rebellious, but also very disorganized! Paco, her crazy pet chameleon, is always in her pocket.

Tom: Very cool, but also very clumsy. He is crazy in love with Vic, who is not interested in him at all.

Ed: A little cold and mysterious at first glance, but actually a very nice guy and a talented dancer!

Iris Berrens: The founder of our school. We admire her a lot, even though she can be tough on her students.

Khan: Our yoga teacher. He's handsome and super laid-back—definitely our best teacher. I am crazy about him!

Table of Contents

Chapter
1

A Mysterious Phone Call

"**I** mean, they're hilarious, but watching them is exhausting! I spent all Saturday and Sunday playing hide and seek, building forts out of sheets, telling them stories, playing dress-up. I was so relieved when their parents came home!"

Vic sits cross-legged on her bed, telling us about her crazy new babysitting job. She spent the whole weekend watching twin six-year-olds. I'm sure she's tired, but now she has two fifty dollar bills on her bedside table.

"So, what are you going to do with all that money?" asks Lena.

Vic smiles greedily.

"I don't know yet. I saw the cutest pair of white jeans in a shop window the other day, but there was also an adorable blue skirt . . ."

I shake my head. I should've known—Vic is obsessed with fashion. She would sell her own bed to buy the latest trendy jacket. Lena strokes Paco on the head and he blinks contentedly. I glance at my alarm clock. Whoa, it'll go off any second; I better get going.

I get up.

"Hey guys, it's my turn to take a shower!"

I should introduce myself: my name is Zoe. Zoe Myer. I live in the dorms at Groove High. Yes, that's right . . . the great dance school founded by Iris Berrens, legendary ballerina, after the death of her husband, the choreographer Alexx Berrens.

Vic, Lena, and I share a room. All three of us are freshmen at Groove High.

I've known Vic since we were seven years old, and we became friends with Lena at our very first audition. That same day we met Paco. He's unusual at our school—he can't dance at all. In fact, he has no talent other than catching dead bugs with his sticky tongue, which is his favorite pastime. Don't worry, Paco's not an alien. He's Lena's pet chameleon. She loves him and refuses to be separated from him. But

animals are strictly prohibited at Groove, so Paco is a stowaway.

Tom is the clown of our group of friends. Among his many talents is an incredible gift for imitation. He makes us die laughing with his impressions of Miss Nakamura, or David, her little follower, or Kim, our worst enemy. Poor Tom has two major flaws: his clumsiness and the fact that he's so innocent. To make things worse, he's crazy in love with Vic.

He would do anything for her. In return, my beautiful friend, who has absolutely no intention of going out with him, takes advantage of him.

Maybe opposites do attract. After all, Ed is part of

our group, and he's the absolute antithesis of Tom. He's dark, reserved, and always dressed like a model. His father is none other than the world-renowned choreographer Philippe Kauffman. Ed spends most of his time practicing. If he's not in class, we'll find him in the dance hall, working on his form, practicing his arabesques and jumps until they are perfect. He's the only one of us who doesn't live in a dorm at school. He lives with his father and little brother, Kevin, in a huge, glamorous apartment downtown.

Earlier this year, the five of us decided to create *Groove Zine*, an indie magazine about stuff that happens at our school. Ms. Genet, the librarian, lets us use a room in the school library, which we now call our newsroom.

"Come on, let's go get breakfast," I say. My stomach rumbles like a volcano about to erupt.

"So what have you been up to this weekend?" Vic asks us, picking at a piece of bread.

Vic always picks at her food. You'll never see her eat any other way. She claims she has to pay attention to her figure, but she's as thin as a rail! I don't know how she does it. Me, I'm always hungry. The menu at Groove High, which is specially designed by a dietician to limit our calories, never fills me up. Not Vic. She's is always turning down dessert!

"Oh, you know," answers Lena quietly. "I went to Ed's to hang out and we went for a walk. Sunday I just lazed around."

"Lazing around," sighs Vic. "I'm so jealous!"

I rolled my eyes. Vic, the hyperactive social butterfly, lazing around? That would never happen. She can never sit still—a typical Pisces.

I guess I haven't mentioned that I'm an amateur astrologer. I've done charts for all my friends.

"Actually," Vic went on, "what I really want right now is . . ."

Dancin' in the sky!

Vic's Threatz ring tone interrupts her in the middle of her sentence. I'm not into rap, but that's Vic's taste in music.

"Hello? Yes . . ."

Vic's eyes widen. She gets up and leaves the table, cell phone glued to her ear.

"Yes, of course," we hear her say.

Lena looks at me.

"Who is it?"

I shrug.

"Her parents maybe? I hope it's not bad news . . ."

Vic has left the cafeteria. The double doors fly behind her. From the next table, Kim and her group of nasty friends give us dirty looks. As usual.

I'm a little worried. I have a bad feeling about this. Vic never acts so secretive. Tom, on the other hand, does not seem worried. He puts a second chocolate-covered cookie in his mouth. This gives him a perfect chocolate mustache. Too bad Vic isn't here to admire it—I bet it would improve his chances with her!

The hands of the clock drag slowly on. Students are dropping off their trays and leaving the cafeteria. Only a few minutes till class. There's still no sign of Vic.

Suddenly the door opens.

"Where have you been? I've been waiting in the courtyard for fifteen minutes!"

It's not Vic, but Ed, impeccable as usual in red, slightly flared trousers, and a fitted v-neck pullover.

I bite my lip. Where's Vic? It's not like her to ditch us. I stand up reluctantly, hoping everything's okay. The bell rings. We have no choice but to go. In the courtyard, all the students stand in a perfectly straight line. Nakamura, a.k.a. "The Dragon," rallies her troops and calls the roll.

Miss Nakamura. How can I describe her? She's

Dean of Students, and calling the roll is a duty she takes very seriously. The legend is that before working here, she was the commanding officer for an elite squad of soldiers in the Japanese Army. She always keeps a close watch on the Groove Team— Vic, Lena, Ed, Tom, and me. We try to stay under her radar, but nothing escapes her eye.

"You again!" she cries as she sees us coming. "You never miss a chance to be late."

We get in line, keeping our heads down. One of our basic rules: at all costs, do not make Nakamura mad at you!

That's when I see Vic. She's already in line, staring into space. Within seconds, I switch from concern to anger. She left us in the cafeteria with no explanation!

I walk up to her. "Psst, Vic."

She jumps at the sound of my voice.

"What?"

"Hey, we were waiting for you and . . ."

"You were? Oh, sorry."

But this doesn't sound like a real apology. I'm not ready to let her off so easily.

"Who was on the phone?"

Vic tucks a lock of hair behind her ear. She always does this when she is nervous or anxious.

"Um, it was my cousin."

"Elizabeth?"

Vic and I have known each other forever, so I've met most of her family. She shakes her head.

"No, not Elizabeth. You don't know this cousin."

"Okay," I say, "why was this cousin . . ."

"Miss Myer!"

Nakamura is planted in front of me, ready to spit flames! In a tiny voice, I say, "Yes, Miss . . ."

"Can you explain to me how . . ."

Riiiiiing!

Phew! Literally saved by the bell. Without stopping to ask permission, I disappear into the crowd and manage to avoid the wrath of Nakamura.

But I don't forget about the unfinished conversation with Vic. There's something she's not telling me, but believe me, I will get to the bottom of this!

Flying and a Lucky Crash

"**P**lease, you guys! Quiet! We'll get into major trouble!"

Poor Jeremy stands at the podium, trying to speak over the chattering crowd. We're all in our French classroom. It's 1:15, and Miss Brunette is still not here. She's never late.

"Please, you guys," Jeremy shouts again.

Jeremy tries so hard, but he has no ability to inspire fear like Nakamura. It's like comparing Sponge Bob to Lord Voldemort. He yells at the top of his lungs, but nothing works. The students chat away, already sure that Jeremy is here to tell us Miss Brunette can't make it to class today. That means two hours of freedom!

"Miss Brunette will not be coming . . ." Jeremy begins.

The response is immediate: laughter, cheers of joy . . .

"Don't worry," Jeremy says, "she's a little sick, but it is nothing serious."

I shake my head. Does he really think we are listening?

"Instead of French class . . ."

Moans of disappointment—and he hasn't even finished his sentence.

"We'll have a yoga class with Mr. Khan."

Awesome! I don't know about the others, but I couldn't be happier. Two hours of yoga with my favorite teacher is a thousand times better than two hours of French class.

"It's too cold to have class outdoors, so Mr. Khan asks you to join him in the gym."

We move into the hall in a compact group. Too bad the fall weather keeps us inside—when it's nice out, Mr. Khan holds class in the field behind the school, which used to be a football field. According to him, being close to nature promotes meditation. Kim disagrees and always complains that sitting in the grass may damage her outrageously expensive tracksuit. She totally misses the point that yoga teaches you to detach yourself from material things.

I have to tell you a little more about Mr. Khan. He's an amazing teacher. In fact, he's the coolest, most attentive, most charming, most adorable, most . . . everything in the whole school. I wish he could trade places with Iris Berrens, who is constantly criticizing me. I don't know why, but I feel like she focuses on me more than anyone else! Khan, on the other hand, is nothing but encouraging. I had never done yoga before, but he has converted me. For the past two weeks, I've been getting up every morning—okay, when I don't

sleep in—I take a few minutes to do my Sun Salutations. Vic and Lena laugh at me, of course, but I find it really helps clear my head. And Khan thinks it's great.

Khan is not his real name. He mentioned it once, but his real name is almost impossible to pronounce. So we call him by his nickname. He's from India, and he sometimes tells us about his country. When he speaks about India, he looks off into the distance and his voice becomes even softer and warmer. He talks about the years he spent in Calcutta with a master yoga instructor. I've heard that India can be a beautiful, spiritual place. My dream is to travel there!

"Come on, get your mats!"

Khan greets us with a smile. He wears a white tunic and pants that highlight his dark skin and black eyes. Did I mention that he's incredibly handsome? As usual, I sit up front so I can see everything he does . . . and so he'll be sure to see me! We sit waiting on our multicolored mats while Khan takes the lotus position. I try to do it too.

"Is everyone doing well this morning?" he asks in his mesmerizing voice.

We don't speak, but nod quietly, as we are sup-posed to. The silence is . . .

"Lame! I polished my toes yesterday and they're already chipped!" shouts Kim

She's the only person who would dare to open her mouth as we begin a meditation. A sharp "shush"—from Lena—silences her.

"Put your hands on your knees," Khan continues, "and completely relax your back."

His voice has a magical effect on me. I feel my-self transforming into vapor. My mind becomes lighter than a cloud. I don't care if people think it's strange—I feel like I could fly!

I close my eyes . . .

Class is over before I know it. We're rolling up our mats when all at once, Iris Berrens, our director, bursts into the gym.

"Khan? Can I see you for a minute?"

"Of course, Iris. I'm all yours."

For some reason, I feel a pinch in my heart every time I see Khan and Iris together . . . and now, in addition to the pinch, I feel Lena elbowing me in the ribs.

"What?"

"Do you see how Khan looks at Iris Berrens?"

"No, why?"

"Take a look . . ."

I look. At first I don't notice anything unusual . . . true, Iris Berrens, who is always so severe, seems to relax in Khan's presence. In fact, I never see her smile except when she's with him . . .

"He's devouring her with his eyes," Lena whispers.

What is she talking about? Sure, Khan's eyes are very bright, but he looks at everyone like that, right?

"Trust me, Zoe, I can always tell. Khan is crazy in love with Iris Berrens!"

I shake my head but don't speak. Why should I listen to Lena anyway? What does she know?

"So how's your cousin?"

Chemistry class. The teacher sits behind her desk preparing an explosive mixture. She looks a little doubtful. As a precaution, I steer clear of the front row.

Vic spent our entire free period on the phone.

Yes, again. And yet again, she has walked off so no one can hear her conversation. When she comes back, just before the bell, she intentionally avoids looking at me. But I don't let it go. Leaning forward at my desk, I whisper, "Which cousin is this?"

Without lifting her eyes, Vic says, "Mi— Michaela is her name."

"Really? How old is she?"

"About seventeen."

"A long lost cousin, huh?"

Vic finally turns, looking irritated.

"What do you want, Zoe?" she whispers. "You want us to get two hours in detention? If that's what you want, keep talking."

I glance at the teacher, who is too absorbed in her chemicals to notice us. In a low voice, I reply, "Look, I'm worried about you, that's all. You won't tell me what's going on . . ."

Vic sighs in exasperation.

"Why can't you just leave me alone for once? You're always on my back! I wish you'd just forget I exist."

I'm speechless. Vic turns her chair so all I can see is her back. She wishes I'd forget her? Fine. If that's what she wants. Perfect! I know you too well, Vic. I also turn my chair. Back against back, we ignore each other.

A tiny ball of paper lands on my desk. Only Lena could've thrown such a perfect shot. She's a basketball champ. I unfold the paper and read:

What are you and Vic fighting about?

On the back of the note, I write:

Her mysterious phone calls. I'll explain after class.

I throw the paper back. But I'm no basketball player. Instead of landing gently on Lena's desk, my shot bounces to the left, hits the floor, and comes to rest right at Kim's feet. Of course, she leans down to grab the note. I clench my fists. I hate her. She unfolds the note, naturally trying to figure out the best way to get me and Lena in trouble. Then she taps Angie on the shoulder and whispers something in her ear. Angie, super quiet,

turns to me. She plucks the note from Kim's hand and places it neatly on the chemistry teacher's desk.

I'm busted. And just last week Iris Berrens gave me a detention because I forgot my tights! Here I go again. I'll have to spend my afternoon locked up with Jeremy instead of going shopping in the city. My only consolation is that Lena and Vic will probably be there with me. Detention for Vic! This will be the first time in her life! She'll want to kill me!

I sneak a look at the teacher. She's so busy that she doesn't seem to notice the note. Suddenly—a miracle!—she knocks over one of her precious beakers! Fizzy liquid chemicals flood the table and turn my note into unreadable pulp.

I realize I haven't breathed in almost two minutes.

I'm ready to scream at Kim, but I play it cool till the end of class.

Imprisoned in the Girls' Bathroom

"**S**he's hiding something, that's for sure!"

We're sitting in an empty study room. Lena caresses Paco, who sleeps in her lap. I sit across from her. Vic, who is still fuming at me, has left for a study session to prepare for a test tomorrow. Tom and Ed sit on either side of me.

"Why won't she tell us who she's talking to?" Lena continues.

"Especially you, Zoe. You know her better than any of us. Hey, do you think it's a family problem?"

I shrug.

"I have no idea. It's impossible to figure out."

A thought crosses my mind: maybe it's not so impossible. I pull out my cell phone and calmly call Vic's parents.

Two rings. It's 6:30, and normally they'd be eating

dinner at home.

"Hello?"

"Hello . . . Mrs. Solis?"

"Yes?"

"I'm sorry, Mrs. Solis, I hit the wrong number. I meant to call my parents. It's Zoe . . ."

"Oh, Zoe! How are you? It's good to hear from you, Sweetie. How's everything going? Is Vic okay?"

"Yes, she's fine."

"It's sweet of you to call your parents, Zoe. Vic hardly ever calls us. It's been two weeks since I even heard her voice."

"I'll tell her to call you, Mrs. Solis. Well, I guess I should call my parents . . ."

"Say hello to them for me. Bye, Zoe."

"I will. Bye, Mrs. Solis."

I hang up. Ed, Tom, and Lena stare at me.

"So?" Lena prods.

I slowly shake my head.

"I guess it's not a family thing. She hasn't even talked to her parents for two weeks."

Silence.

"Okay, we need to think," Lena says.

"Maybe it's an old boyfriend," Tom suggests

quietly.

I shake my head.

"Vic's never had a boyfriend."

Tom is obviously relieved, but not for long.

"But maybe she has one now," I say. "Maybe that's where she was all weekend."

"I thought she was babysitting." Lena looks surprised.

I shrug.

"Maybe that's just what she told us."

Tom looks heartbroken. He hates to think of Vic with someone else. But this theory makes more sense than anything else we've thought of.

Lena bites the inside of her cheek.

"I know!" she says. "Let's just borrow her cell phone and listen to her messages. This mystery caller has probably left at least one . . ."

"Let's just leave her alone," Ed says suddenly. "She has a right to her privacy, right?"

This is the first time he has spoken all afternoon. I have to admit, he has a point. But then again . . .

"Privacy!" Lena explodes. "You think we're just doing this for fun? If she wants to have little secrets, fine, but we're her friends and we're worried about her."

Hmm. This doesn't make perfect sense. I feel I should add to the argument.

"Ed, you have to understand, we don't want to let Vic down. If she has a problem she can't talk about, we have to find another way to help her."

"Why do you assume it's a problem?" Ed asks.

"If it wasn't a problem, she'd tell us about it," Lena insists. "So it's settled. We'll find a way to take her phone without her noticing . . ."

And just like that, we have a plan.

On my way into our room, I bump into Khan and Miss Berrens. They are standing in the lobby, deep in conversation. What if Lena is right? What if Khan is in love with Iris Berrens? No, no, that's impossible. Except now I see that Khan just put his hand on Iris's shoulder. Tenderly. Yes, tenderly. There's no other word for it. I can't bear to see this. I walk faster and am at our door in just a few seconds.

I'm scouting out the area, to make sure we safely accomplish our mission. Lena joins me a moment later.

I open the door.

Vic is in our room, studying. I know I will have to apologize if I want the plan to work.

"Hey, Vic . . ."

"What?"

She doesn't lift her head.

"Um, I . . . I . . ."

Arrgh! It's so hard to apologize.

"I'm-sorry-for-what-happened-during-chemistry-can-we-be-friends-again?"

I blurt it all out in one breath, trying to get it over with. Vic takes her time. Slowly, she lifts up her pencil, looks at the wall, finally turns to me . . .

"It's fine."

Phew. It worked. She can be so stubborn, some-times—believe me, I know!

I decide to change the subject.

"So . . . have you noticed something going on

between Khan and Iris Berrens?"

Why did I bring that up? Why didn't I say, "it was cool missing French class," or something like that?

Vic frowns.

"Why do you ask?"

As if she doesn't know!

"Lena keeps saying that Khan is in love with Iris Berrens."

"Obviously."

"What?"

"Yes, of course," she repeats. "Khan is in love with Iris, and Iris is in love with Khan. Except they don't want anyone to know."

"How do you know?" I stammer. "Anyway, Iris was madly in love with her husband. When he died, she was heartbroken."

"But that was ten years ago, Zoe. It couldn't be more obvious that she's in love with Khan now. Just look at them when they're together. Khan devours Iris with his eyes . . ."

She uses the same words Lena used earlier.

". . . and she's usually so strict, but when he's around, she's completely relaxed."

I've noticed this too.

"But that doesn't prove it!"

I don't know what came over me. I didn't mean to shout.

Vic shakes her head.

"Oh, poor Zoe . . ."

"What do you mean, 'poor Zoe'?"

"You're in love with Khan. But he's your teacher, and you're just a freshman."

She must be insane!

"I am not in love with Khan!"

"Zoe, I know you better than I know myself. Look, you have to stop fantasizing about the yoga teacher. You'll only get hurt."

Whatever! It's true that Vic knows me, but that doesn't mean she knows everything. As if!

I am about to tell her off when the door opens and Lena walks in.

"Hi guys," she says cheerfully.

Vic and I face each other like two cowboys in the old West. Lena glances at me conspiratorially. The mission! I almost forgot. I have to calm down. I look at Vic's desk. No cell phone. Not on her bedside table, either. Oh, there it is. Carelessly thrown on her quilt.

Lena follows my gaze and spots the phone. Vic turns back to her homework.

Lena coughs to get Vic's attention. "Hey, what are you working on?"

Oh no! Lena is not exactly an Oscar-quality actress. Vic can tell something is weird. Why would Lena suddenly be so interested in her work?

"Why do you ask?"

Lena tries to act nonchalant—okay, she fails miserably at acting nonchalant—and takes a few steps toward Vic.

"Oh, well, you know, I just . . ."

Vic squints.

"What's up with you two? You're acting really weird."

Lena drops onto Vic's bed. This is the moment of truth. If our friend yells, "Hey! Don't touch my cell phone!" our mission falls apart. But she doesn't say anything. She just keeps looking coolly at Lena. I have to do something.

"We're acting weird?" I ask. "We're completely normal. You're the one being weird!"

Vic turns and looks at me. From the corner of my eye, I see Lena's arm moving as she closes her hand over the cell phone.

"It's true! You never stop working. You spend all your time in this room . . ."

I stand in front of Lena and put my hands behind my back.

"All you care about is your grades, Vic! It worries me. You should . . ."

Lena slips the cell phone into my hands. I quickly stash it in the back pocket of my jeans.

"You should get out, have fun, think about something else for once!"

"I just spent the whole weekend away from school!"

I smile stupidly, standing next to Lena.

"Oh, that's right. I forgot. You're right, Vic! You know how I am, I always get worked up over nothing. Whoops, I promised Tom I'd go listen to his new guitar song. See you, girls!"

I run to the door, but before it closes behind me I hear Vic say, "Is she even crazier than usual, or is it just me?"

I rush down the hall and into the girls' bathroom. Tom is waiting in the first stall on the right. When I join him, he sits on the closed toilet, legs folded and feet off the floor so no one will see his skater shoes—size 11—under the stall door.

"So?" he asks.

"Shhh," I say.

I call Vic's voicemail and glue the phone to my ear.

"You have no new messages and one saved message," the recording says. "Saved message."

I hold my breath.

"Hello Vic . . ."

It's a guy's voice. Our suspicions are confirmed, but the sound is terrible. Static makes it almost impossible to understand.

". . . I really want to thank you for understanding and listening. Thank you for being there. I'll give you a big hug when I see you . . ."

"So?" Tom says again, increasingly anxious.

How do I tell him without breaking his heart?

"Well . . ."

I should just do it quickly, like ripping off a big adhesive bandage.

"It sounds like there's a boy. Apparently, they're very close."

Tom closes his eyes. He's totally miserable. Unfortunately, there's no time to comfort him. I have to get Vic's cell phone back in our room before she notices it's gone. I put my hand on Tom's shoulder.

"Hey," I say, "maybe it's just a friend."

"Wrong," he says gloomily. "What guy would be 'just friends' with Vic?"

I don't have an answer.

"Look, Tom, I'll go out first. If the coast is clear, I'll whistle and you can follow me, okay?"

Tom shrugs helplessly.

I push the door and immediately hear:

"Oh, look who it is. Miss Tacky."

Kim, Angie, and Clarisse. What horrible timing! If they suspect that I asked Tom to meet me in the bathroom, they'll definitely tell Nakamura, and I'll be totally humiliated! I need to make sure Tom has heard them enter. As loudly as possible, I say, "Oh, hi, Kim. Hi, Angie. Hi, Clarisse."

The three girls glare at me like I'm crazy. I hope their surprise visit ends soon. Tom might be stuck in here for a long time. Kim and her clique use this bathroom as their headquarters, and sometimes they're in here for hours!

I feel awful for Tom. But what can I do?

Chapter 4

A New Scheme Blossoms

Just when you think it can't get worse, something else goes wrong. On my way back to the room, I run into Kim's brother, Luke.

Luke is definitely a cool guy at school. In fact, some people call him Luke "Ladies Man" Vandenberg. He's extremely popular and just as fickle. Since the beginning of the year, he's changed girlfriends at least four times! He's the kind of boy who knows he's hot and is unbearably smug about it. Also, he and his friend Zachary run the Capoeira Club, where the members practice a combination of Brazilian martial arts and dance. It adds to their status, as you can imagine. Vic, who's susceptible to this kind of charm, fell madly in love with him at first sight. Just like almost every girl in school. Lena and I are the only ones who didn't fall hard for him. In fact, I hate him. He makes a habit of treating me like I'm four years old, so I'm always nervous when he's around. Why can't he resist tormenting me?

"Hey! Hi, Carrot Top!"

Like this. I can't stand it. Especially because I'm not redheaded at all, I'm strawberry blonde!

"Want to go for a walk?"

I slip Vic's cell phone into the pocket of my jeans and shake my head. Luke keeps walking, but doesn't forget to ruffle my hair as he passes.

"Don't forget your homework, Carrot Top!" he calls as he walks away.

Grrr!

But I ignore him. I need to hurry.

I walk in to find Lena and Vic tearing the room apart. Vic always tries to keep our room clean and well-organized, which isn't easy with roommates like Lena and me. But now everything is upside down. Vic is under the bed. Lena moves around some papers on her desk.

I stand frozen in the doorway.

"What are you doing?"

Lena shoots me a look before responding.

"Vic has just lost her cell phone. She can't find it anywhere!"

It takes me a couple of seconds to understand the situation. Vic lost her cell phone? Her cell phone is in my pocket!

"Don't panic!" I exclaim. "I'll help you. It has to be here somewhere."

Do I feel guilty about stealing my friend's cell phone and then lying about it blatantly so that she thinks she lost it herself?

Nope! Not at all. It's all going to be okay.

Vic is carefully unmaking her bed. She shakes her quilt, turns the pillowcase inside out . . .

"I'm sure I put it here, I'm sure of it," she mumbles.

I walk up to her desk, move the chair aside, and pretend to be looking as I slip the phone from my pocket and put it on the floor. It's still in my hands when . . .

Dancin' in the sky!

Vic jumps as if she's been stuck with a pin.

"Where is it?" she cries.

Yikes. Vic always acts like she's so in control of her emotions. But now, she dives for the cell phone, which is still in my hand.

"I just saw it under your desk," I stutter. "It must

49

have fallen . . ."

But Vic doesn't care.

"Hello," she answers.

A smile blooms across her face.

"Yes! Hold on just a sec . . ."

And without so much as a glance at Lena and me,
she rushes out of the room, phone glued to her ear.

I shiver at the thought that the phone could've started ringing while it was still in my pocket. What would I have said?

"Did you see the glorious look on her face when she answered the phone?" Lena crows. "Now we know it's definitely not a family problem."

I drop onto my bed.

"Yeah, and she had a message. From a boy."

Lena is blown away.

"Vic has a boyfriend, and she hasn't even bothered to mention it! To us, her best friends!"

I shake my head.

"I guess that's what's going on."

"There's something fishy about this," Lena exclaims. "Why would she hide a boyfriend?"

"I have no idea!"

"Well, I'll get to the bottom of this," she says. "Believe me!"

It's 8:00 P.M. Jeremy let us spend the evening here in the library until 9:30. We convinced him we needed to work on *Groove Zine*. He loves our little magazine, so that was easy. "But you have to promise not to cause problems," he said. "Can I trust you?"

"Of course, Jeremy!"

Vic is still working back in our dorm room. The rest of us sit around the table listening to Tom.

"One hour," he says. "I was in there a whole hour. Can you imagine?"

I bite my lip. Yes, I can imagine him balancing on the toilet, not breathing for fear of being seen by Kim and her clique.

"It was horrible," he says. "Somebody put on perfume. The smell drifted up, and I almost choked trying to stop from sneezing."

Lena leans onto my shoulder to stifle her laughter. I hope she doesn't offend Tom—he can be sensitive. And this is not a good time for him, considering what we've figured out about Vic.

"On the bright side, I heard everything Kim said," he adds.

"Oh, that should be thrilling," Lena says sarcastically.

"Actually, it was," Tom says. "They were talking about Khan and Iris Berrens."

Wait a minute. This I want to hear.

"What did they say?"

Tom shrugs. "Oh, it's dumb. They said Khan asked

Iris to marry him."

My heart leaps in my chest. My stomach tightens. Can this be true?

"I'm not surprised," Ed says slowly.

What? My eyes practically pop out of their sockets. Lena smiles triumphantly and adds, "See, Zoe, I told you Khan was in love with Iris! I have a flair for this sort of thing."

I keep my mouth shut. I don't think I could speak even if I wanted to. Vic's words replay in my head: You are in love with Khan, Zoe! No, no, no! This is stupid. I'm just a freshman and he . . . he is the best teacher, the most brilliant, most knowledgeable, most fun, most . . . Oh no! I have to stop this right now!

"Why doesn't it surprise you?" Tom asks Ed.

"My father went to school with Khan and Iris," Ed says. "He says Khan has always been in love with Iris."

That much I knew.

Not that Khan was in love with Iris, but that they had all gone to school together. I read it on the Internet when I was researching Philippe Kauffman.

I may not have mentioned it, but I'm a huge fan of Philippe Kauffman and his work. To me, he is the greatest choreographer of our time. His imagination seems to renew itself constantly. He is always reinventing the art of dance, and his ballets are full of magic and power. The first time I saw one of his productions, I knew I wanted to become a choreographer, and that was when I was only five years old. Since then, none of my feelings about his brilliance have changed. In my mind, Kauffman is on the highest artistic pedestal imaginable! But, he's on a lower pedestal as a human being. After I actually met him, I accepted that he is more complicated than just a marble idol.

"Iris's parents moved here from Czechoslovakia," Ed goes on. "They didn't have the money to send her to a top school. But she was quickly spotted by an agent who helped her get a scholarship at the prestigious Fame Academy in New York."

I put my elbows on the table and rest my chin in my hands. I already know part of Iris's story, but

I've missed some of the pieces. And Ed's voice is so relaxing. I didn't know that Iris came from a family with a modest background and went to school on scholarship. I can't help remembering that Vic is in the same situation at Groove High.

"She arrived in the U.S. when she was thirteen," Ed continues, as if telling a fairy tale. "Khan arrived around the same time. My father joined the Fame Academy with him. Khan and Iris immediately became very close. Khan came from India. He was an orphan, and his career was very difficult. They supported each other a lot. According to my father, they were inseparable for four years. He never saw Iris without Khan or Kahn without Iris. He also told me that Iris was very playful when she was young, even a little bit of a rebel."

I don't need to close my eyes to picture the young Iris and Khan together, sharing all of their joys and pains. Strangely, I did not even find it hard to imagine her as cheerful and mischievous, even though she's so stern and severe now.

"One day, Alexx Berrens, the choreographer, came to an audition at the Fame Academy. He was looking for a dancer for his ballet. My father says it was love at first sight for Alexx and Iris. At first glance, he fell in love with this young dancer who was so talented. He begged her to go with him. Initially, she refused because she wanted to finish her studies."

How romantic!

"But Alexx didn't give up. Each day, Iris received huge bouquets of flowers, jewelry, dresses. He began to create roles for her in his dances. And Iris, who was in love with him too, finally gave in. She immediately became very famous. Journalists said she seemed to fly above the stage. Everything was wonderful for almost eight years. And then. . . . Well, you know the rest."

He's right. Everyone knows what happened after that. Alexx Berrens died in a motorcycle accident. Iris never returned to the stage. She dropped out of the public eye for more than a year, until she founded Groove High.

"And where was Khan all this time?" Lena asked. "What was he doing while Iris was with her husband? He must have been terribly upset, right?"

Ed shrugs.

"Khan stayed at Fame another year after Iris left. Then he returned to India for a while. But he never lost track of Iris. They stayed good friends. And Khan and Alexx always got along well."

I shake my head.

"How is that possible? How could he become friends with the man who took away the woman he loved?"

"I asked my father the same thing," Ed replies. "He

explained that Khan just wanted Iris to be happy. And Alexx made her happy. He also said yoga and meditation probably helped Khan to accept it all."

I shake my head.

"I guess."

We sit in silence for a moment, thinking about the story of Iris, Khan, and Alexx. Contradictory thoughts

collide in our heads—Khan and Iris, Iris and Khan.

"We should help!" Lena cries suddenly.

"What?" Tom asks, startled.

"We should help," she repeats. "Khan and Iris! Their story is so romantic!"

"How?" I ask.

"We know that Khan asked Iris to marry him . . ." Lena says.

"We know that's what Kim says," Ed interrupts. "But that's not quite the same as knowing it's true."

Lena dismisses this.

"What we don't know is whether Iris will accept. Maybe she still loves Alexx Berrens. Maybe she's afraid of letting go of his memory. But living in the past won't make her happy, and it keeps Khan from being happy too!"

Tom shakes his head.

"So how do you want to . . . help?"

Lena squints.

"I'm not sure yet, but I'll think about it tonight. I'll let you know in the morning!"

I look at my watch. Quarter after nine already! I get up. It's time for bed. Ed and Lena get up too.

"Wait!" Tom calls in a desperate voice.

"What?" Lena asks.

"What about Vic?"

Lena raises her eyebrows.

"Hmmm. Vic? Well, it's simple. Step one: espionage. We must try to gather as much information as possible. We must, for example, eavesdrop on her conversations. That's the only way we'll find out who this mysterious stranger is, and why she wants to hide him from us! Agreed?"

Ed, Tom, and I nod.

"So," Lena concludes. "The meeting is adjourned!"

The Groove High Emergency

I had a strange dream last night. When Lena and I got back to our room, Vic was already in bed asleep. The phone rested on her bedside table. I put on my pajamas, and as soon as I got in bed, I sank into a deep sleep, full of strange dreams. Paco had a role, as he often does. I was at a wedding. There were many people, and at the front stood the bride and groom. Their backs were turned so I couldn't see their faces. I tried to break through the crowd to approach them, but it was very difficult. Then I found a shortcut through the girls' bathroom, where I found Tom having tea with Kim. When I finally got close enough to the married couple, I saw that the groom was Khan, but I still couldn't see the woman because her face was covered with a veil. Khan looked at her and gently lifted the veil . . . and the bride was Paco! I was amazed. Especially when Paco began to sing:

Dancin' in the sky!

I woke up, startled.

I rubbed my eyes and there was Vic, her hair mussed from sleep, with her phone glued to her ear. Her ring tone had woken me from my dream. I kept my eyes closed, but I listened. Though I was barely awake, I hadn't forgotten Lena's advice: espionage!

Vic spoke in a whisper.

"Yes . . . I don't know . . . it's not easy. If I can, I'll arrange it. Don't worry . . . you can count on me, we'll be able to . . ."

My heart was beating so fast I thought it would explode. Vic was planning a secret rendezvous with her boyfriend! I couldn't wait to tell the gang . . .

I spread the news after breakfast, as soon as I was alone with Tom, Lena, and Ed. Tom was devastated. Even more than the day before. He chewed on his nails so viciously I was afraid he was about to bite his fingers.

Ed had spoken to his father that evening, and his father confirmed the story about Khan's proposal, adding that if Iris refused, Khan would probably not remain at Groove High.

"My father explained that they created Groove High together," Ed said. "Iris was in mourning and unable to cope. Khan was the one who helped her get the school going. But if Iris rejects him, he feels he won't be able to work with her anymore. Groove High will close!"

We were horrified. This was serious. Where would we go if Groove High closed? Tom turned to Lena.

"Got any ideas?"

Lena frowned and tipped her head to the side.

"Well, maybe we could try . . ."

"People!"

Nakamura! As always, she arrived at the worst possible time.

"Did you not hear the bell?" she shouted.

The bell? Who cared about the bell when Groove High was in danger?

"Go line up!" she yelled.

We didn't need to hear it twice. We weren't going to wait around for her to start spitting fire.

Now it's 10:00. We are taking our break outdoors.

We're a little tired after our music class—Mr. Carter, the teacher, talked about Bach for two hours! Don't get me wrong; I love Bach. Bach is beautiful. But two hours! Luckily, he finished with a piece of fascinating rock music none of us had heard before. Mr. Carter is great. The first time I walked into his class, I was afraid it would be lame. He looks like something from an earlier century with his small, pointed beard, suit with tails, and top hat. His taste in fashion is definitely from another time. But his taste in music is clearly contemporary. He surfs the Internet to research amazing groups from all over the world. Right now he's into Korean rock.

But that's beside the point. We have more important things to worry about. And I'm not talking about the

Khan-Iris drama, I'm talking about Vic! So far, so good. Her phone has remained in her pocket and has not rung once. I look around the courtyard. On the other side, Kim is hanging out with her followers. Or should I say Princess Kim and her handmaidens? A few feet away, Luke stands with his friend Zach . . . why are they looking at us? He waves in our direction. What does this mean? Oh, well. He takes out his cell phone and hits the key pad . . .

Dancin' in the sky!

I freeze.

Luke has barely put his phone to his ear when I hear Vic's voice. Quick as lightning, Vic has her phone at her ear and is hurrying away from our group. I barely have time to hear her mutter, "Yes, okay. Don't worry . . ."

I'm blown away! Vic and Luke. Luke and Vic. So he is my friend's mysterious boyfriend? Of course, that voice mail on her cell phone. It was hard to make out the voice, but now I'm sure it was Luke. How had I not recognized it earlier? Now I see why Vic refuses to tell us about her boyfriend!

The whole thing is suddenly obvious. Vic has had a crush on him since the first day of school!

This is crazy! What should we do now?

We call an emergency meeting. But we can't meet till the end of the day. Our fine arts class is a total disaster. The professor asks us to make a statue using nothing but geometric shapes. It can be abstract or realistic. "Let yourself be led by your imagination," he says, and we try to obey.

But my imagination is blank—I can't concentrate. I make the first thing that comes into my head. Believe it or not, the first thing that comes is Paco. But how do you make a chameleon out of geometric shapes? When I finish, the teacher walks behind me and stops to look at my work.

"This is excellent," he says. "Perfect! You truly let your imagination guide you, without worrying about reality."

That isn't what I intend, but hey, if the art teacher likes it . . .

Our group is quiet at lunch. Vic barely says two words. And I am furious, imagining that the whole time she is thinking about Luke.

How has she gotten him not to make fun of her?

Luke spends all his time flirting with anything that moves. He's a horrible macho guy who changes girlfriends as often as he changes his shirt! Exactly the kind of guy that should be avoided at all costs.

Next we have an hour of math, an hour of geography, and an hour of English. Nothing to report. When we go outdoors again, I am responsible for keeping an eye on Vic, and Tom is supposed to monitor Luke.

Tom shares a room with Zach and Luke. When school started, all the rooms for freshman boys were full, but there was an extra spot in a room of juniors. At first, Tom was super intimidated by the older boys, but gradually he's gotten used to them. I know that Zach and Luke treat him like a buddy. Sometimes Zach lets Tom play guitar with him, and Luke offered to let him join the Capoeira Club.

This situation is perfect. Tom is able to hang out with them and spy. But maybe Luke knows better than to call Vic while Tom is within earshot. Or maybe the two lovebirds aren't in the mood to coo to each other. Whatever the reason, right now their cell phones remain in their pockets.

We've slipped away from Vic and are gathered in an empty study room with Jeremy's permission. We're not doing any news writing, though. Everyone

is a little nervous—if Vic comes looking for us, this is the first place she'll try.

"Well, what do we do?"

It's Lena who asks the question. Tom continues to gnaw on what's left of his nails. He shakes his head.

"Luke Vandenberg! Vic is going out with Luke Vandenberg! This is horrible, just horrible!"

"Maybe we should just talk to Vic directly," Ed suggests. "We can tell her it's a bad idea to date a guy like Luke. He'll make fun of her, and then he'll dump her just like he's dumped all his other girlfriends."

I shrug.

"She already knows that! She's seen how he acts. But I'm sure she's somehow convinced it will be different with her, that she'll be the one he actually cares about, that he'll change . . ."

"From what I know of Vic," Lena interrupts, "the more we tell her not to do something, the more she'll want to do it."

She's not wrong. Vic has a major stubborn streak. She always wants to prove herself right.

"Well, what if we speak directly to Luke?" Ed asks.

The rest of us look at him. He must be insane.

"Are you kidding?" Lena exclaims. "He'll laugh in our faces! No, the only thing to do is set a trap. Maybe we can set something up where Luke flirts with a girl and Vic sees it happen. That'll prove to her that she can't trust him."

"It's a good idea," Ed nods. "But what girl? Who would play along with us?"

Lena thinks for a moment. Suddenly her gaze is fixed on me.

"What if Zoe . . ." she begins.

What? Oh no, what is she thinking? I don't let her finish.

"No way! I'm not going to flirt with Luke Vandenberg!"

Lena rolls her eyes in exasperation. "I'm not asking you to flirt with Luke, Zoe! Anyway, it would never work. You're not his type."

I'm weird sometimes. A second earlier, I'd have rather died than speak to Luke Vandenberg. But now that Lena says I'm not his type, I almost want to prove her wrong. Anyway, why would she say I'm not his type? Because I'm strawberry blonde (not a redhead!)? Because I'm not pretty enough? Is that it? What does Lena know about my powers of seduction? I am about to open my mouth and make a huge mistake that I would've regretted immediately—like saying, "I'll show you! I'll have Luke on his knees begging to go out with me!"—but luckily, Lena keeps talking.

"No, I was thinking we could write a letter from a secret admirer. The secret admirer will ask Luke to meet her somewhere. Then we get Vic into the same place at the same time, and if Luke shows up, Vic will see that she can't trust him!"

She's a genius! What a clever plan! Much better than me trying to bat my eyes at Luke while he calls me "Carrot Top."

"This is where you come in, Zoe. Of the four of us, you have the most imagination. You'll have no problem writing the letter."

I nod. "I'm in," I say.

"While we're at it," she continues, "we should also write one for Khan and one for Iris."

Ed frowns.

"What for?"

Lena smiles mischievously. Clearly the wheels are turning in her head.

"I've been thinking—we've got to do something to help them. After all, maybe Iris wants to marry Khan and just doesn't want to admit it."

Ed still doesn't understand.

"And then?"

"And then, if we create a romantic moment and they meet face-to-face, Iris might let down her guard . . ."

Lena is clever, very clever. I've got to go. Off to write three love letters. That's going to be much more fun than trigonometry homework. Plus, I have another idea. I'm going to read Iris's and Khan's horoscopes. I'll find out their Zodiac signs and whether they are compatible. Then I'll add the predictions to spice up the letters!

Ed goes home and Lena hurries off to feed Paco before dinner. Meanwhile, Tom and I move slowly toward the cafeteria.

"You know," Tom says, looking at his fingernails. There's nothing left to chew. "I can't think of anything else but Vic and . . . him, but I love her more than ever."

"I know, Tom. I feel awful too. To think that Vic's

going out with Luke Vandenberg . . ."

I don't finish my sentence. Footsteps echo in the hall in front of us, and I see someone's shadow. We realize a person is running away at full speed.

Someone is listening to us!

But who?

The Stars Align

"Astral profile of Iris Berrens:

Date of birth: March 23, in the sign of Venus and the moon.

Astrological sign: Aries.

Stone: Amber.

Dominant characteristics: Stubborn and tenacious. Knows how to keep her objectives. A worker. Ambitious. Demanding with herself and with others. Very sensitive. Romantic. Faithful in love. Can be cold and withdrawn."

"This is crazy," Tom says. "That's exactly her!"

"Well, you know, I didn't have a lot of time," I say. "If I had more information, I could've made it more complete . . ."

Lena did the research on the Internet yesterday evening. After dinner, she asked Jeremy for the keys to the computer lab, saying she needed to work on a very important paper for school. Jeremy agreed, even though he knows that on Wednesdays we have dancing all morning. Jeremy is just so nice that he can't refuse us anything.

Lena figured out where Iris and Khan were born and on what dates. This helped me figure out most of their astral charts. I was missing an important piece of information: time of birth. But I don't see how I could go up to one of my teachers and ask, "Hey, what time were you born?"

This morning, Tom courageously risked his life—of course, I mean risked getting caught by Nakamura—to sneak into the girls' dorm and join us in our room. When Vic saw him, she groaned and then went and

locked herself in the bathroom. She has never liked Tom coming into our room in the morning. She is in the shower, but we still talk quietly, in case she can hear us over the water. After all, we haven't told her about the Iris-Khan situation.

"Read Khan's profile now," Lena presses impatiently.

"Astral profile of Khan:

Date of birth: January 12, in the sign of Mars and the sun.

Astrological sign: Capricorn.

Stone: Granite.

Dominant characteristics: A good balance between the practical and spiritual. Excellent listener. Sensitive. Tolerant. Knows what he wants and cannot be easily upset. Faithful in love and friendship. Loves to learn and transmit his knowledge. At the same time, close to the earth and sky."

"That sounds just like him, too," Tom says, truly impressed.

I smile at my third piece of paper. I worked on this until late last night!

"Now I'll read about their compatibility," I say.

"Balance of love between Khan and Iris Berrens:

Stars: The moon and sun are opposites. It is difficult to imagine a relationship between two stars that never intersect. However, Mars and Venus provide another aspect: these two stars perfectly complement each other, and they allow the sun and the moon to meet. Therefore, this match is quite positive. We can also note the dominant characteristics they have in common: sensitivity and faithfulness. These points are very important for a couple in lasting love. On the other hand, if we look closely . . ."

"So, are we going to breakfast or camping out here?"

The door of the bathroom has suddenly opened and Vic stands there, impeccably dressed as usual. I crumple the paper in my hand. Vic seems not to notice. Obviously, she has other things on her mind, like meeting up with her darling Luke in the cafeteria. But just you wait, my dear! Not only have I written up the astral profiles, I've also written a love letter for your boyfriend. I'm sorry in advance, Vic, because I know this is going to be hard. But it's for your own good!

I slip the papers into my pocket and follow Tom and Lena after Vic.

I head for breakfast—and I'm starving!

I immediately notice Luke. He's sitting in his usual place, at the far end of the cafeteria with his best friend, Zach. We asked Tom to keep an eye on him during the evening, but he couldn't be with him every minute. At Groove High, juniors have a later curfew, and apparently Zach and Luke spent two hours shooting hoops on the basketball court last night. When they returned, Tom was already fast asleep. Oh well. Tom will be able to catch up if he's sneaky enough.

While Vic, Lena, and I sit down, Tom goes over to hang out with Luke. I can't help but notice the hateful look Kim shoots him.

Why does she look so upset? We're used to her mean looks, but this time it's different, as if . . . I'm not sure. I see Tom out of the corner of my eye. He's acting natural. I'm not sure what he says to Luke, but I see his hand deftly slide the folded note into Luke's leather jacket. Perfect move, Tom!

But we have a problem if Kim's been watching the whole time. I bet my first tutu she saw him put the letter in Luke's jacket!

Arrgh! I can already feel the pain she will send our way.

It will be a shame if our plan falls apart. Especially because I'm pretty proud of my letter. Here's what it said:

My love,
(I had trouble thinking of a good salutation. Just plain "Luke" seemed a little dry. "Light of my life" was a little too cheesy. But "my love" is classic. The perfect tone.)
Just seeing you pass by makes my heart pound. But it's not enough. (Notice how I set the tone first, and wait till later to ask for the meeting?) *I must meet with you and tell you how I feel. It torments me to keep my feelings inside.* (I put that in because it sounds super romantic to me.) *Meet me tonight in the gym at 6:00.* (After a lot of thought, I decided not to include a signature. It's more sophisticated that way.)

So, what do you think? Perfect, right?
However, writing letters as if Iris Berrens and Khan

were writing them was a totally different story. I needed a model, so I used the acceptance letter I received from Groove High, which Iris Berrens wrote by hand. I had it neatly folded and tucked into the pages of my journal. Lena helped me out by getting (I have no idea how) a sports equipment order written by Khan. (She probably found it by digging in Petula Anderson's office. She's Iris Berrens's secretary, who says we can call her "Grandma." She's so sweet that she lets us get away with anything.)

It took time to imitate their handwriting, but I'm pretty proud of the final product.

First, the letter to Iris Berrens:

Iris,
(I have chosen to make the greeting very simple. Khan would not be too sentimental—after all, he's a Capricorn.) *I absolutely must talk to you face-to-face tonight. It is extremely important. Meet me at the gym at 6:30.* (I know, I know, we will have to make sure that we get Luke and Vic out of there in less than half an hour! But we had no choice. At 7:00, we have to be back in the dorms. We decided to have everyone go to the same place so we

didn't have to run back and forth.)

Yours always,

(I heard someone say this in a movie once.)

Khan

Then the letter to Khan:

Khan,

I have given much thought to your proposal. You managed to find the words to convince me. Let's talk about it this evening, face-to-face in the gym at 6:30.

Your Iris

This is simple, effective, impeccable! It's very Aries; it gets straight to the point. I knew that astrology would come in handy someday!

Lena and I left breakfast, saying we needed to feed Paco. We snuck into the empty teachers' lounge and dropped the letters in Khan's and Iris Berrens's mailboxes.

Don't worry, no one saw us. We checked at least twenty times. And we returned just in time for the bell. Nakamura couldn't even yell at us.

"Miss Myer, you're slouching!"

I straighten with a sigh. I told you: Iris Berrens is always on my back. Both literally and figuratively.

"Miss Myer, your pointe shoes!"

And on Wednesday morning, we have four hours of dance class! Now, as I bend to fix my dance shoes, I wonder if we really did the right thing, helping her get together with Khan . . . the handsomest, coolest, nicest . . .

"Ouch!"

"Miss Solis, what are you doing with your legs?"

Vic has fallen to her knees on the floor. She rubs her calf. Behind her, Angie, Kim, and Clarisse snicker. I think they sound demonic.

"In the center, people," Iris orders, without worrying about Vic. "Show me the sequence we worked on yesterday. Mr. Muller, you go first."

Tom goes into the second position. Arched arm above his head, he raises his right leg very tensely. We are practicing without music, which is difficult. We must keep the same pace. Jumps, arabesques, always keeping our balance. Tom is doing pretty well. But the final step is composed of a royale. Tom has never managed to complete that jump and correctly end in the fifth position, especially not at the end of a sequence.

"That's enough, Mr. Muller. Miss Robertson, you next!"

Lena has great potential, but constantly has to practice keeping her feet pointed and her arms in the right position.

"You lack grace, Miss Robertson. Grace and precision. Miss Solis, you!"

Vic is the best dancer of all of us. She raises her arms, keeping her body perfectly straight. Meanwhile, Angie kneels and pretends to adjust the ribbon of her pointe shoe. As Vic begins to move into her sequence, Angie grabs her ankle and Vic collapses to the floor for the second time. Angie is already standing up again; Iris has seen nothing. Clarisse has been distracting her so that Angie can get away with it.

Looking up from Clarisse, Iris discovers Vic on the floor. My friend holds her knee. She seems to be in terrible pain. We gather around her. If she has broken something, it might mean the end of her career. Iris Berrens squats near Vic.

"Where does it hurt?"

"My knee!" Vic groans, tears in her eyes.

I am dying to expose Angie's part in this, but I know it's useless. She'll deny it, and I will end up blaming a classmate without proof.

Iris Berrens touches Vic's knee.

"I don't think it's serious," she says. "We shall see if it becomes swollen. Miss Myer, please take your friend to the nurse's office."

She doesn't even have to ask. All the bad feelings between Vic and me disappear as if by magic. When your dream is to become a professional dancer, an injury like this is very serious. I turn to Kim and her toadies, and it takes everything in me not to knock them silly. Kim glares at me and whispers maliciously:

"Your girlfriend better leave my brother alone. Got it?"

My mouth drops open. But suddenly it all makes sense.

The spy I heard running down the hall last night was one of Kim's groupies. She must have heard me talking about Vic and Luke with Tom! She doesn't want Vic anywhere near her brother.

I knew it. Kim knows how to retaliate. And the situation is getting more complicated by the minute.

Vic's Secret

We walk down the hallway to the infirmary.

Vic limps, leaning on me in order to walk. And she is fuming.

"You saw, Zoe! You saw what they did to me!"

"Yes, I saw. They deserve payback, and don't worry, the Groove Team won't let them get away with this!"

Vic shakes her head.

"But why are they doing this? They're always rotten to us, but they've never gone this far. And why me?"

I bite my lip. This might be a good time to talk to her about what's happening.

"Well . . . actually, I think Kim's upset . . . because you're dating her brother!"

"What?"

Vic stops and looks at me with her blue eyes wide as dinner plates.

"What are you talking about? I'm not going out with Luke! Sure, I'd love to go out with him, but he barely even looks at me!"

I sigh.

"There's no point in lying, Vic, we already know everything."

"You know everything? What do you know? What are you talking about?"

"We know that you and Luke talk on the phone several times a day, and that you're in love with him!"

Vic bursts out laughing.

"We talk on the phone several times a day? What makes you think that?"

I don't answer. Vic wouldn't keep lying like this, but then what . . .

"Well, you've been getting a lot of phone calls, and . . ."

"Zoe, Zoe, Zoe!"

Vic puts her hand on her forehead and leads me to a bench.

"Come on, let's sit down."

"We have to take you to the nurse's office."

"That can wait. We need to talk. I guess I'll finally let you in the story."

I sit down next to Vic, and in her slightly mocking voice, she explains everything. It's incredible. We are totally wrong. Vic has not been dating Luke. She's not having a secret romance at all. The phone calls are about something else entirely. Only she has not wanted to tell us.

Vic feels better after a little massage, cream, a bandage, and some crutches. "Only until the end of the week," the nurse says. "Your knee is badly bruised, and by using crutches you will give it a chance to heal. After that, you should be able to dance again."

At noon, in the study room, Kim comes to talk to us. Very proudly, she shows us a letter, which I recognize immediately as the one I wrote for Luke. The little witch has managed to steal it from her brother's pocket.

She waves it in Vic's face, then slowly, methodically tears it into four pieces.

"My brother would never even look at a girl like you, Victoria Solis," she hisses. "And if I see you come near him again, you'll regret it!"

Then Kim becomes very confused as we all laugh at her.

Once she's gone, Vic takes out her mobile phone and punches in a number.

"Michael? Hello? Yes, it's all set up for this afternoon. Yes. Please come. It's no trouble. My friends all want to meet you. We're very excited."

Tom beams at me. He couldn't be happier.

We sit in the cafeteria, waiting to meet Michael for the first time. Michael, the guy who's been calling Vic since the beginning of the week. It turns out she hasn't been lying as much as I thought. Michael is her cousin, a cousin she hasn't seen in five years.

It turned out to be just a coincidence that Luke had his phone at his ear the other day when Vic happened to receive a call from Michael—a coincidence that I completely misinterpreted!

Vic told us all about her cousin and explained why she'd tried so hard to keep it a secret. We laughed, and Lena was almost in tears.

"You still should have trusted us!"

Vic said that she wasn't sure she could trust schemers like Lena and me with any secret. After all, we had secretly called her mother, snatched her cell phone, and who knows what else. We had to admit we probably would have tried to "help" and somehow managed to give away the big secret! Lena grinned, and Ed reassured Vic, saying he understood and thought Michael sounded fantastic. Tom was so happy and relieved, he couldn't speak. When he found out Vic wasn't in love after all, his world was rosy once again. He leaped and executed a perfect royale. Then it was Vic who rolled her eyes.

"Take it easy, Tom!"

Now she stands up. "There he is," she calls.

We turn to see a young man with a shadow of a beard, slim, smiling, and rolling in on his wheelchair. Vic balances on her crutches and waves.

This was Vic's secret!

Michael is twenty-three now, but he had left home after arguing with his parents—Vic's aunt and uncle—who disagreed with Michael's plans for the future. When he was seventeen, Michael was in a terrible car accident, and his parents reacted by being extremely protective. He knew his parents had good intentions, but he felt smothered. When he was accepted into an art school in San Francisco, Michael knew it was the chance of a lifetime. He left home and headed west. Back in New York, his parents worked hard to pay for Michael's tuition while raising Michael's younger brother and sister. Over the years, his parents had never been able make the long trip to visit him.

At the art school, Michael discovered his real talent as a cartoonist, and in the last year he'd created a cartoon character with a disability. Now, a large newspaper group had offered Michael a contract. Soon, his cartoons would run each week in newspapers across the country. Michael wanted to surprise his whole family and tell them the big news in person, so he contacted his cousin Vic to help him.

"Hello, everyone!"
Michael holds out his hand. He's grinning.
"It's great to meet Vic's friends. I'm so lucky she is there for me. This will be a fantastic surprise for

my family. Vic is helping to make it all possible. She even lent me some of her babysitting money for the airfare. But I'm not worried about being able to repay her now!"

Vic told us how she had arranged to make sure Michael's family would be gathered at home on Friday evening so she could bring Michael and surprise them.

We chat for a long time. Michael has a wacky sense of humor and lots of stories about the art world in San Francisco. He shows us some of his cartoons, which are hilarious. We hardly notice the time passing . . . but we do notice vengeful Kim passing. She has crossed the cafeteria at least five times this afternoon, throwing mean looks at us. I don't let her know it, but inwardly I'm gloating. She seems so curious about our new friend. Wait till she finds out he's a famous cartoonist!

Suddenly, Lena nudges me with her elbow.

Iris Berrens is coming toward us. My heart skips a beat. But it's okay, she's smiling. She reaches out to Michael.

"I am delighted to meet you. Miss Solis has told me your wonderful news, and I wanted to personally congratulate you."

"Thank you," Michael replies. "It's great that you're letting me stay tonight at Groove High."

"We're delighted, Michael. And I think you are an excellent example of how talent and determination can bring real success. And thank you for agreeing to speak to our students tomorrow about future careers in art."

With these words, Iris nods at us and walks away.

"She's as impressive as you said, Vic," says Michael. "You guys are lucky."

That's when I remember the secret rendezvous. I glance at my watch and quickly stand up.

"It's quarter after six! We have less than fifteen minutes to get the gym ready!"

Lena and I planned to light a few candles to help create a romantic atmosphere. Lena and I had put them into my bag this morning. We can still pull it off.

"What are you talking about?" Vic asks, surprised.

Of course! We haven't told her anything about our plan.

"Come on, we'll explain. Let's go!"

Zoe Hears the News

We light a dozen candles, and everything looks wonderful. Our plan can only succeed. Once we explain our plan to Vic, she thinks it is a great idea. Michael laughs and agrees to help us.

We're just about to sneak out of the gym, when we hear . . .

Voices! Just outside the gym! We have no choice but to rush into the bathroom. Poor Tom, he's been through this before.

"What's going on?"

We hear Iris Berrens's voice. Is she alone? I can't resist the urge to peek. I open the door a crack. No, Khan is with her. Our plan is working!

Khan looks at the candles and smiles. Lena pushes me out of the way so she can see, too. Tom pokes his head to one side, and Vic and Ed do the same on the other side. We may be witnessing a crucial moment in a beautiful love story . . .

"I can't believe they did all this," Khan smiles.

"What were they thinking?" Iris sighs.

"They wanted to do something nice."

Squeezed tight against each other, Ed, Lena, Tom, Vic, and I are petrified. Our plan hasn't worked at all—Khan and Iris knew immediately that it was a trick. They've come only to figure out what we've been up to. Our only hope is that they don't know who wrote those letters. Otherwise, we're in major trouble!

"Who do you think is behind it?" Iris asks.

Khan smiles and shrugs.

"I'd put my money on Zoe, Tom, Lena, and the rest of their group. They're the only ones who'd dream up something like this."

Okay, game's over. We're caught!

"What do they call themselves?"

"The Groove Team," Iris answers. "And you're right, they have no shortage of ideas."

Khan sits on the bleachers. Iris sits beside him.

"Zoe Myer in particular seems to have a great

imagination."

Khan shakes his head.

"She definitely has quite a personality. But they all do."

"I know, but especially her. I do push her every day."

She sure does!

"It's only because I see so much passion, creativity, and originality in her. I've never seen that in any other student. In fact, it reminds me . . ."

"Of Alexx."

Khan finishes Iris's sentence for her. I don't know what to think. So Iris doesn't pick on me because

she hates me. She really believes in me.

"Yes," Iris says. "I think she'll make an excellent choreographer."

Khan puts his hands on Iris's shoulders. We all hold our breath. Iris looks at Khan and shakes her head.

"Khan, no," she whispers.

Khan gently takes her arm.

They stand together and blow out the candles, side by side. Without another word, they leave the gymnasium.

Michael and Vic leave early this afternoon. In the morning, the Groove Team had announced to Vic that she needed to do more for Michael.

"You have to tell your parents why you've been so busy. And demand that they organize a family reunion party right away and invite your other cousins, uncles, and aunts to celebrate Michael's visit," Lena insisted.

Vic saw the brilliance of her friends' suggestion and launched the plans. Her parents are already e-mailing everyone with arrangements. And the Groove Team has decided to create a special ballet and perform it at the party. The starring role features a ballerina who does an unusual part while on crutches!

And me? I feel absolutely amazing after hearing what Iris said about me. It makes me want to work like crazy to prove that she is right about me, that someday I'll be a great choreographer.

We also understand now that Khan is in love with Iris, but she does not feel ready yet. After reflecting a little—with no need to look at their astrological profiles—I decide that they'd be an ideal couple. Lena has a new scheme that is supposed to "help" Iris decide. She hasn't told me yet, but I'm not sure I want to hear . . .

As far as Kim is concerned—you can be sure we did not let her get away with anything. Not after what she did to Vic.

Ed called a Japanese restaurant from his father's house downtown. He ordered fifty pieces of sushi for delivery.

We know that Kim loves sushi, and we wanted to offer her a "small gift." Unfortunately, by a "terrible mistake," Vic put the sushi on a bench while Kim was putting on her tutu. Just then, Lena happened to run into Kim and . . . oops! . . . they bumped each other so hard that Kim fell . . . right onto the bench full of sushi! Poor thing! Her beautiful tutu was covered in slimy, squishy raw fish! But it still looked pretty, with all those bright green, pink, and black smears!

Kim had to run back to her room to change, so she arrived late to class. She tried to explain to Iris Berrens, who is very strict about being on time. Iris didn't want to hear Kim's excuses. She simply suggested that Kim take it easy on the sushi for a while.

Kim looked ready to explode.

It was perfect!

About the Author

Amélie Sarn: Amélie has two major flaws: excessive curiosity and a tendency to gorge herself. Not just on food, but on reading, travel, games, children, friends, and anything that makes her laugh. This gives her lots of material for stories! When her publisher asked her to write the stories of Zoe and the Groove Team, she revealed her dark side. Of all the characters in *Groove High*, she admits that her favorite is Kim!

About the Illustrator

Virgile Trouillot: With his feet on the ground, but his head forever in the clouds, Virgile spent his youth under the constant influence of cartoons, manga, and other comics.

When he's not illustrating *Groove High* Books, Virgile develops animated series for *Planet Nemo*. Virgile spends time in his own version of a city zoo that's right in his apartment. His non-human companions include an army of ninja chinchillas that he has raised himself and many insects that science has not yet identified.

Web Sites

In order to ensure the safety and currency of recommended Internet links, Windmill maintains and updates an online list of sites. To access links to learn more about the *Groove High* characters and their adventures, please go to www.windmillbooks.com/weblinks and select this book's title.

For more great fiction and nonfiction, go to www.windmillbooks.com.